You Can Be a DOCTOR

Doctors work in offices or at hospitals. When people are hurt or sick, doctors help them get well. Doctors fix broken bones and take out tonsils. Doctors give people check-ups and sometimes shots, so that they won't get sick.

You Can Be a POLICE OFFICER

Police officers work in police stations, in cars, on motorcycles—even on horseback! They patrol the streets and help protect people. Police officers direct traffic, give tickets to speeders—and sometimes arrest criminals.

You Can Be a LETTER CARRIER

Letter carriers work in every city and town, bringing mail to homes and offices. There is a lot to carry, and the mail can be heavy! Letter carriers usually have to work in all kinds of weather—even rain and snow.

You Can Be an ARTIST

Artists draw and paint pictures. Some do this for books and magazines, and some create cartoons for TV or newspapers. Some paint pictures of people, called portraits. Artists get ideas from the world around them, and they use their imaginations!

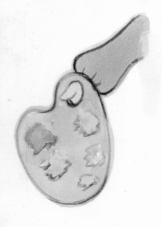

You Can Be a FIRE FIGHTER

Fire fighters work wherever there are fires. At the fire stations, they wait for an alarm. When it comes, they rush off in big trucks to put out the fire. Fire fighters climb tall ladders and handle powerful hoses.

You Can Be a TEACHER

Teachers work at schools. They help children learn to count, to read and to write. Teachers like to answer questions and help children to know about many things. They show how to play games, draw pictures and sing songs.

You Can Be a DENTIST

Dentists help keep people's teeth and gums healthy. They clean teeth, take X-rays to find cavities, and fill the cavities. Sometimes a dentist must pull out a decayed tooth. Dentists tell people, "Brush after every meal!"

You Can Be a TV NEWSCASTER

Newscasters work in TV studios. They tell people watching TV what is going on in their own city and all over the world. Sometimes newscasters go where exciting things are happening, and report the news right there!

You Can Be a SINGER

Singers entertain people on TV and radio, in concerts and shows. Some sing with a band. Some, called soloists, sing by themselves, while others are a part of a group. Sometimes singers work in a recording studio, making records and tapes.

You Can Be a SALESPERSON

A salesperson often works in a
store. Good salespeople know
about the items for sale, and can
answer customers' questions.
When a customer buys something,
a salesperson takes the money at the
cash register—and says, "Thank you!"